my friendly neighborhood

Police Officer

Published in the United States of America by Cherry Lake Publishing
Ann Arbor, Michigan
www.cherrylakepublishing.com

Reading Adviser: Marla Conn MS, Ed., Literacy specialist, Read-Ability, Inc.
Book Design: Jennifer Wahi
Illustrator: Jeff Bane

Photo Credits: © John Roman Images / Shutterstock.com, 5; © Philip Lange / Shutterstock.com, 7; © Anne Kitzman / Shutterstock.com, 9; © Stefano Panzeri / Shutterstock.com, 11; © Paolo Bona / Shutterstock.com, 13; © Dmitry Kalinovsky / Shutterstock.com, 15; © Fotosr52 / Shutterstock.com, 17; © Photographee.eu / Shutterstock.com, 19; © Frances A. Miller / Shutterstock.com, 21; © Stuart Monk / Shutterstock.com, 23; © aleksandr-mansurov-ru, 2-3, 24; Cover, 1, 10, 18, 20, Jeff Bane

Library of Congress Cataloging-in-Publication Data

Names: Bell, Samantha, author.
Title: Police officer / Samantha Bell.
Description: Ann Arbor : Cherry Lake Publishing, [2017] | Series: My friendly neighborhood | Audience: K to Grade 3. | Includes bibliographical references and index.
Identifiers: LCCN 2016056584| ISBN 9781634728263 (hardcover) | ISBN 9781634729154 (pdf) | ISBN 9781534100046 (pbk.) | ISBN 9781534100930 (hosted ebook)
Subjects: LCSH: Police--Juvenile literature.
Classification: LCC HV7922 .B45 2017 | DDC 363.2/3--dc23
LC record available at https://lccn.loc.gov/2016056584

Printed in the United States of America
Corporate Graphics

table of contents

About the author: Samantha Bell has written and illustrated over 60 books for children. She lives in South Carolina with her family and pets. She is very thankful for the helpers in her community.

About the illustrator: Jeff Bane and his two business partners own a studio along the American River in Folsom, California, home of the 1849 Gold Rush. When Jeff's not sketching or illustrating for clients, he's either swimming or kayaking in the river to relax.

Police officers **protect** us.
They help us follow the law.

What are some ways you follow the law?

Some officers ride on motorcycles. Some ride in cars. Some ride on horses.

DALLAS POLICE
111
DALLAS POLICE

The police keep the roads safe.
They make drivers slow down.
They stop bad drivers.

POLICE

Sometimes there is a car **accident**. Police officers come to help. They direct **traffic**.

Some officers work in a neighborhood.

Some officers work in a school.

Police officers help people. They help in a fire or **flood**.

Has a police officer ever helped you?

How?

Police officers stop **criminals**. They arrest them.

SPECIAL
POLICE

Some officers work with dogs. The dogs are trained. They help find people who are lost.

Police officers keep us safe.

What would you like to
ask a police officer?

glossary & index

glossary

accident (AK-si-duhnt) an unlucky and unplanned event often caused by a mistake

criminals (KRIM-uh-nuhls) people who carry out crimes

flood (FLUHD) water that rises and spreads over the land

protect (pruh-TEKT) to guard or keep something safe from harm, attack, or injury

traffic (TRAF-ik) the cars and other vehicles on the road

index